This book dedicated to my
second grade students;
past, present and future.

In Memory of my mom Bertha M. Shy.
You would be proud!

To request permissions, contact the publisher at
shyglaspublishingllc@gmail.com

ISBN 978-0-578-90427-6

Permission to use material from other works
illustrations by OniOnime
cover design by OniOnime

Printed in the United States of America

Published by Shyglas Publishing, LLC
PO Box 2572 Laurel, Maryland, 20709
shyglaspublishingllc@gmail.com

Are you ready for Second Grade?

Written by
Celisa Shy-Glasper

Illustrated by
OniOnime

Mae was in second-grade. On the first day of school, she felt super smart, and joyful. However, when she returned home, she wore a big frown and sounded grouchy.

Mae took a deep breath.
"Second-grade is no fun, Mom — really!" Mae explained, sounding overwhelmed. "My teacher, Ms. Shy, has a bunch of stupid rules. And, if I'm to get one of her sparkly stickers, I have to follow them — all of them!"

Mom invited Mae to sit with her on the couch in the family room. "Having class rules is great," said Mom casually.

"And sparkly stickers sound awesome! "Sounds to me like you have the best second-grade teacher."

"Yeah, well" said Mae, poorly. "It's not so awesome when I'm the only one in the whole second-grade who didn't get a sticker, today."

"I see," said Mom curiously, and nodding her head. "Now, why do you think that is the case?"

An anxious Mae spoke, "I seriously waited like forever for this one girl to give an answer in Math. It became so hard to wait, honestly. I knew the answer, so I kind of shouted it out."

Mae folded her arms and puckered her lips.

"Well", said Mom, "it sounds like you took away that girl's chance to show how smart she is for second-grade."

"Oh," said Mae slowly. "So that's why the girl looked so mad, and Ms. Shy said I needed to have more self-control for second-grade. Go figure!"

Mom sat closer to Mae.
She told her, "Self-control is super important, and a
big deal in second-grade, Mae."
"If you can learn to be disciplined in class, like
waiting your turn, you will learn many new and great
lessons, as well as enjoy school a lot more!

Mae breathed heavily.
"I think I understand better, Mom!" said Mae.
In first grade, it was — well, different!"

"Yes," said Mom. "Second grade is different in many more ways. You are older now, and so you must be more responsible for your actions and emotions."

"I guess," said Mae, sounding regretful. I was trying to show that I am smart in Math, but I only made it seem like I don't really know how to behave in second-grade – like I'm not ready."

"It's all right, Mae," Mom told her. I understand. "I want you to try not to worry about looking smart all the time. Try more self-control in class tomorrow, and see if that makes everyone happier, Okay?"

Mae agreed. That night in bed, she thought about everything that her mom had said. It would be awesome if she could get one of Ms. Shy's sparkly stickers. If only she could be more responsible.

Just before she fell asleep, she
made a promise.

"I will wait my turn in class,"
she whispered. "I will show
self-control like a true second-
grader."

The next day at school, Mae was more than anxious to test her promise. When class started, she sat quietly, and listened to the teacher.

When Ms. Shy asked her a question, Mae raised her shoulders high, and spoke up confidently. Then, she listened while others took turns. It felt great to her, being responsible.

Not once did Mae break her
promise — even when she came
very close.

The teacher smiled at her all
throughout the day.

"Great self-control," she told Mae. Then she stuck a sparkly red sticker beside Mae's name on the behavior reward chart — her very first one.

"Yes! My first sparkly sticker!" whispered Mae, staring at the chart. "I can't wait to get some more."

The whole class cheered for her. She felt like she was learning and growing.

During the usual recital of the class motto, just before dismissal, Mae smiled while reading it with pride.

We are a team
We act responsible
We work together
We help each other
We respect each other
We give praises
We are here to learn
We are smart
We are not bullies
We will always be kind
We will never give up
Because
We are shining stars!

Aa Bb Cc Dd Ee Ff Gg Hh Ii Jj Kk Ll Mm Nn Oo Pp Qq Rr Ss Tt Uu Vv Ww Xx Yy Zz

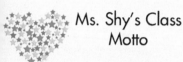

Ms. Shy's Class Motto

In This Class

We are a team
We act responsible
We work together
We help each other
We respect each other
We give praises
We are here to learn
We are smart
We are not bullies
We will always be kind
We will never give up
Because
We are shining stars!

When the last bell went, Mae stopped to talk to the teacher

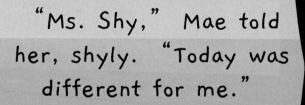

"Ms. Shy," Mae told her, shyly. "Today was different for me."

"I can see that, Mae," the teacher said proudly. "Welcome to second-grade where we keep learning and growing great expectations!"

Aa Bb Cc Dd Ee Ff Gg Hh Ii Jj Kk Ll Mm
Nn Oo Pp Qq Rr Ss Tt Uu Vv Ww Xx Yy Zz

Ms. Shy handed her a sheet of paper.

"Here's a list of a few things that you'll need to learn," she explained to Mae. "Everyone in class has the same list. If you can meet them, there will be plenty more sparkly stickers for you this year."

"I will," Mae promised, smiling. "I know I can!"

She stuck the sheet of paper in her backpack. She could not wait to tell her mother about everything.

"Mom!" Mae shouted from the front door as she reached home. "I had the best second day, ever."

She ripped open her backpack and pulled out the sheet of paper to show Mom.

"I need to work on all of those expectations, Mom," she explained. "It's what second-graders do."

"That's great!" Mom said, smiling. "I believe in you."

"And the best part," said Mae, "is that I have already started being better at the very first one — self-control. I earned four sparkly stickers today!"

"Yeah!" Mom shouted. "You did it. And, I can see that the second expectation says independence. Any plans yet?"

"Sure have," Mae boasted. "I plan to do today's homework all by myself — for the first time.

"Sounds like a good plan toward independence," says Mom.

"Yeah, Mom," Mae amused herself. "A second-grader, like me, has to be independent the sooner the better!

They shared a big laugh.

"I am so proud of you," Mom told her.

"You know what, Mom," said Mae as she headed upstairs, "Second-grade is awesome!"

Made in the USA
Middletown, DE
23 August 2021